FER SHURR!
HOW TO BE A
VALLEY GIRL
—TOTALLY!

BY MARY COREY
AND
VICTORIA WESTERMARK

BANTAM BOOKS
TORONTO · NEW YORK · LONDON · SYDNEY

The authors wish to acknowledge the invaluable help of Tiffany T. of Encino, who shared her knowledge of Valspeak with us.

FER SHURR! HOW TO BE A VALLEY GIRL—TOTALLY!
A Bantam Book/November 1982

Illustrated by Ron Wing

Book Design by James Alfred Gitz

ISBN 0-553-23237-1

Published simultaneously in the United States and Canada

PRINTED IN THE UNITED STATES OF AMERICA

0 9 8 7 6 5 4 3 2 1

WAY RAD CONTENTS

A to Z Glossary of Valspeak
Val Body Language
Gnarly Valley Names
Clothes: Bitchen and Joanie
The Tubular Tube
Valcountry
Some Totally Cool Dudes
Xlnt Lists
No-Sweat Exercise
Valley Girl Vanity License Plates
Buff Valley Bumper Stickers
Cranking Careers
The Hairy
Valley-Girl Diet
The Honorary Vals
The Ultimate Val Test
Honorary Val Diploma

A TO Z GLOSSARY
OF VALSPEAK

A

Airhead: *n.* person with reduced mental capacities; nincompoop, dumb bunny. Syn. space cadet, jel. "I mean, like Tricia's such a total *airhead*, she's like this house with all the lights on, and like nobody's home, fer shurr!"

All the way live: *adj.* expression suggestive of life or vital energy, often used to describe vigorous or animated festivities; way cranking, party hearty. "So like Andrea's sweet sixteen party was like *all the way live*, like she got this totally bitchen, totally black Rabbit convertible!"

Aqua Velva geek: *n.* extremely distasteful male individual, often a self-described "swinger"; a condominium dweller, recognizable by gold neck chains, exposed chest hair, discount toupee, leisure suit (polyester), black zipper boots. Syn. slimeball, nerd. "Ohmigod, Stacey, OK, like this totally skanky *Aqua Velva geek* tried to pick me up, like he goes, 'Hey babe, let's take a walk on the wild side, and like I go, Gag me with a spoon, slimeball!' "

Awesome: *adj.* amazing and marvelous, absolutely astounding, stupendous, too bitchen for words. "Like, OK, so I saw this totally *awesome* dude at the bonerama checkout, right, like I totally thought it was Rick Springfield."

B

Bag it: *imper.* 1. remove from sight, banish; often used in reference to parts of the body, e.g., *bag your face.* 2. just forget it, drop dead. "So this surf punk goes, 'Like *bag* your face frog breath,' and, ohmigod, like I was totally freaking out!"

Barf me out: *interj.* to respond nega-
tively to a highly unsavory situation;
nauseating, too skanky for words, quite
putrid. Syn. gag me with a spoon.
"Sheryl's mom, like she's a total space
cadet, like *barf me out*, she like made
Sheryl throw her dead beta fish down
the garbage disposal, right?"

Beasty: *adj.* used to describe a person or situation that is repellent either
through physical deformity or lack of
social grace; odious, unsightly, dorky.
Syn. yukky. "Like we went to Dupars
and there are all these *beasty* seventh
grade nerds with nine million zits a-
piece, and they're like ordering chocolate pie, right—they're sooo imma-
ture!"

Beige: *adj.* bland, insipid, boring,
strictly ho hum. [Not to be confused
with ho-ho.] "I mean, like the new sex
education teacher is so *beige*, he's like
giving a lecture on VD and the whole
class is like totally asleep, right?"

Bikini wax: *n.* method of depilating the pubic area considered vastly preferable to shaving (no unsightly Band-Aids on inner thigh). "Omigod, it's been like six WEEKS since my last *bikini wax*, right, and so, OK, I'm like a total gorilla or something."

Billys: *n.* a monetary form of exchange; cash, money, loot, moola. "Like I saw the kill mini, but like I totally don't have the *billys* to buy it cuz like I spent my whole allowance getting my hair streaked."

Bitchen: *adj.* 1. perfectly marvelous, splendid, esteemed. 2. to kill for. Syn. buff. "Like I saw the kill mini, but like I totally don't have the billys to buy it cuz like I spent my whole allowance getting my hair streaked, and then like I see this totally *bitchen* blouse that goes perfectly and like I'm sooo bummed!"

Blitzed: *adj.* highly intoxicated, inebriated, fucked up. Syn. buzzed. "Like this dude was *blitzed* to the max fer shurr, like he bonged this totally rad bule!" [Translation: The guy was stoned because he smoked some very good pot.]

Bogus: *adj.* fraudulent, sham, counterfeit, bullshit. "I mean I'm not stupid or anything, like the nerd offers me this totally *bogus* Cartier watch, I mean like he got it in Tijuana, fer shurr!"

Bondage: *n.* unusual sexual practice involving restraints; often joked about by Vals but never performed. See *leather teddy*. "Me and Courtney slept over at Tami's, and like we call Sean and like put on these sexy voices, and like I say I'm wearing my leather teddy, and he goes, 'Are you into *bondage*?' and like he was cranked, fer shurr!"

Bonerama: *n.* 1. big, bitchen place to spend billys, esp. a shopping mall. 2. a supermarket. "So like my mom drops me off at the *bonerama* to pick up like cold pasta salad, right, so I see this totally awesome dude at the checkout, and like I totally thought it was Rick Springfield, fer shurr!"

Bong: *v.* 1. to smoke any mind altering substance through a water pipe called a bong. 2. to chug beer directly from the keg using a hose and a funnel. "I mean like I totally don't know how Sean was standing up, he like *bonged* half the kegger, and like he was totally green."

Bottom line: *n.* lowest common denominator, fundamental truth, nitty gritty. [Archaic. corporate buzzword] "So like the *bottom line* is my mom goes if I don't clean the cat box every day, I don't get my nose done, gag me, fer shurr!"

Bud: *n.* Cannabis sativa, Mary Jane, dope, pot, marijuana. Syn. bule. "Like this dude was blitzed to the max fer shurr, like he bonged this totally rad *bud.*" [Translation, *see blitzed.*]

Bu fu: *n.* person of the homosexual persuasion. "Jeff was over, and like I wanted to fool around, you know, and like all he wanted to do was like play Pac-Man with my spas little brother, so I go, 'Like what are you, a total *bu fu* or what?'"

Bummed: *adj.* at a low ebb, dejected, in an extremely bad mood, not having a good time. [Hippie, circa 1967: bummer, bum trip] "Ohmigod, like I'm totally *bummed,* OK, like I hide my retainer in the microwave and like my mom like totally melts it."

Buzzed: *adj.* under the influence of controlled and uncontrolled substances; loaded, fucked up. Syn. blitzed. "Like it's not like I'm a total jel or anything, but like these coasters have a couple keggers, OK, and like we got way *buzzed* is all."

C

Cas: *adj.* pronounced *cazh*; informal, casual, like way loose, laid back, mellow. "I mean it's like the funniest when Jeff dresses *cas*, like in shorts, cuz like you can see his cute butt."

Chez: *n.* slender wooden incendiary devices tipped with a chemical substance that produces fire; matches. "So this hodad turns out to be a total crispy, like he plays with *chez*, and you know the geek almost sets my mini on fire."

Coaster: *n.* 1. person living in proximity to the ocean, a total beach person. 2. term usually shouted from cars at barefoot passersby. "Like you know this beasty *coaster* goes, 'You wanna bag some rays?' and like I totally go, 'Bag your face, surf punk.' "

Cool: *adj.* calmly audacious, self-possessed, poised; sangfroid (French). Syn. hot. "So I mean like my new phone is sooo *cool*, like it's totally ivory and like gold, you know, like sooo boudoir!"

Cranking: *adj.* heated or vehement in spirit, clamorous, uproarious; an evolved positive state of achievement, really happening. See *all the way live*. "Ohmigod, the Clash concert was like *cranking* to the max, I mean sooo tubular, like I was way jazzed!"

Credit card: *n.* small card belonging to one's father or mother entitling the bearer to charge merchandise, also known as plastic; usually found in groups. "Like this salesgirl goes, 'This *credit card* is over limit,' and I go, 'Are you totally shurr?' and she goes, 'Let me check,' and she's so lame, she goes, 'Oh, I'm sorry, I looked at the wrong name,' and I'm edged, fer shurr!"

Crill: *adj.* lower than plankton, inferior, totally grody. Syn. skanky. "I could totally freak out, like my mom, the Jell-O head, buys me this *crill* barf-pink terry cloth like strapless dress to wear to Cori's bat mitzvah."

Crispy, crispo: *n.* person with fried brains who has been blitzed out one time too many; a burnout. See *airhead, jel, space cadet.* "The geek was a total *crispy*, OK, like he tried to pour carob chips all over my smoothie."

Cruise: *v.* to conduct an exploration, to stalk, to ferret out cool dudes. "Stacey and I *cruise* the Galleria forever, but like Jeff wasn't there, so I buy this kill polka-dot bow tie, so like we weren't wasting time or anything."

D

Dermatologist: *n.* zit doc, an absolute necessity. "I'm like freaking out, like OK, I've got this grody zit, like the kind that hurts, and like my nerd *dermatologist* is at La Costa for a week!"

Ders: *n.* oral copulation, short for *headers*. "It was a way cranking party, but I was sooo embarrassed, like I walk into the bedroom and Tricia's totally giving Sean *ders*!"

De-Val: *v.* to deprogram a person from Valspeak. [Does not refer to money except for a certain Beverly Hills speech pathologist who is making a lot of billys doing it.] "Ohmigod, I could die, Hillary's parents sent her to this doctor who's supposed to like *de-Val* her, and she's not allowed to say *like*, or *totally*, or anything, gag me!"

Dork: *n.* repellent, cretinous individual; clod. Syn. nerd. "So this *dork* goes, 'Wanna go to a concert?' and I go, 'Fer shurr,' and he goes, 'Like I hope you like Joan Baez,' and I go 'Get serious.' "

Drug faze: *n.* a period of experimentation usually gone through in junior high school. See *bud, blitzed, buzzed, reefdogger.* "You know, like I totally went through my *drug faze* when I was younger, like now I'm into the clean stuff, you know, like facials."

Dude: *n.* male of the extant species of the genus Homo and of the primate family; any guy between the ages of 13 and 40. "Like OK, so this red Porsche pulls up next to me, and so this way gnarly *dude* is totally smiling at me, and like I could totally swear it's Timothy Hutton!"

E

Edged: *adj.* incensed, angry, mad as hell, pissed off. "Like I'm just lying there next to the pool, and my lame little brother throws the car keys into the Jacuzzi, right, and now I'm *edged*, fer shurr!"

F

Fag: *n.* 1. that homosexual gentleman that just left the room. 2. any odious male person regardless of sexual preference, i.e., disco fag, prep fag, punk fag, surf fag, fag fag. "Ohmigod, I mean my *fag* little brother sees Jeff and goes, 'Tiffany's got her period,' and I could totally die."

Fenced: *adj.* See *edged.* [Not to be confused with a barrier around a yard.] "So Andrea scores another ten thousand points on Centipede and beats me, right, and then like I break a nail and I'm *fenced,* fer shurr."

Fer shurr: *interj.* 1. exclamatory affirmative, as in "for sure." 2. contemporary form of hippie slang "right on." "Like, you know, *fer shurr!*"

Fill: *n.* a weekly maintenance process required for all porcelain and acrylic fingernails; a Val must. "My nails are so grody I could barf, like if I don't get a *fill,* I'll totally look like E.T."

Flake: *n.* an unreliable person, noodlehead. See *dork*, *hodad*, *retard*. "So you know, this *flake* tells me he'll like take me to Limbo Night at the country club, and he totally never calls, and like I'm edged!"

Full-sesh: *adv. adj. n.* to be totally engrossing, to go the distance, grooving to the max; all the way. "Tami's Rocky Horror sweet sixteen went *full-sesh*, like we totally threw rice and cards, right, and then we pigged out on chocolate mousse, and like I know I gained ten pounds!"

G

Gag me with a spoon: *vulg.* a strange request; make me vomit. Syn. barf me out. "Like this flake was so totally skanky, OK, like he has yukky green stuff on his braces and he doesn't even know it, like *gag me with a spoon*!"

Galleria: *n.* a way bitchen Sherman Oaks shopping mall, a center of the Val universe. See *bonerama, cruise.* "Like it's so bitchen at the *Galleria*, like today Stacey and me get our ears pierced there, OK, and buy these way rad New Wave earrings, and then we like play Pac-Man."

Geek: *n.* human eyesore, dildo, wimp, jerk; Aqua Velva geek, dork, nerd. "Like I'm at the Sports Center and this *geek* is coming on to me, and he goes, 'Encino means *oak* in Spanish,' and I mean like I could care."

Gnarly: *adj.* 1. exclamatory expression denoting vastness or excellence. 2. humongous, big. Syn. awesome, bitchen. "Like I'm at the Roxy, and this *gnarly* white limo pulls up, and like you won't believe who gets out—it was totally Tom Selleck, ohmigod!"

Goes: *v.* replaces the antiquated verb "to say." "So like I'm on the phone for hours, and finally I *go*, 'You wanna go to Disneyland,' and Jeff *goes*, 'Way bitchen,' and I *go*, 'I'm shurr!'"

Go fer it: *interj.* 1. exclamatory expression implying boundless optimism about life's possibilities. 2. a philosophy popularized by Burt Reynolds and Sylvester Stallone. "So like my plastic surgeon goes, 'You could totally look like Olivia Newton-John if you have your nose done,' and like I asked my dad and he says, '*Go fer it*, Tiffany.'"

Grody: *adj.* disgusting, repugnant, nauseating, gross; used to describe something you would want to squash with your foot. "I'm sitting there, and like this crispo waitress serves me hot tea in a Styrofoam cup, right, and it's like so *grody*, the Styrofoam is melting in the tea, like barf me out!"

GQ: *n.* acronym for *Gentlemen's Quarterly*, a popular magazine of men's fashions; Val girls buy it to look at pictures of cool dudes; Val dudes buy it to dress like the pictures of cool dudes to attract Val girls. "So I loan Whitney my copy of *GQ*, right, and she drops strawberry yogurt right on the cover, and like I could totally be so edged, but I tried to be cool."

H

Hairy: *adj.* difficult, irksome, a big deal. "Like it was sooo *hairy*, this geek that plays with chez sets my mini on fire, and I'm going, 'Fire, fire,' and he tries to put it out, and he like pours Diet Pepsi all over me."

Hi-rider: *n.* male individual who jacks up the rear end of his vehicle for no apparent reason, often found in parking lots at the beach. [Not to be confused with high roller.] "So this lame *hi-rider* like guns his Datsun pickup in the parking lot, right, and like he runs over this blitzed hodad's foot, gross me out, I'm shurr."

Hodad: *n.* 1. male person suffering from surfer delusions, often heard shouting "surf's up." 2. cretin, clown, wimp, phony. See *geek, nerd.* "This *hodad* is so edged, like he stares at his foot for blood and stuff, right, but like, ohmigod, cuz the geek is so buzzed, he doesn't even feel it."

Ho-ho: *n.* female between ages of 13 and 18 who has a tendency to put on weight; self-proclaimed "thunder thighs," fat girl. "I mean like this *ho-ho* is stuffing her face with croissants, right, and I'm eating this incredibly tiny salad, and she totally goes, 'Can I have your tomatoes?' I'm shurr!"

Hot: *adj.* emotionally intense, the ultimate, sensational, sexy. [Archaic. stolen recently, wanted by police.] Syn. cool. "So like I see this totally *hot* black and turquoise leotard at Contempo Casuals, and like I'm so bummed cuz like I can't find my credit card!"

I

I: *pers. pron.* object of self-obsession, as in *me, me, me, me*; the most interesting person in the world. "I can't believe *I* look so bitchen, like *I'm* not beautiful or anything, but like *I* strive for perfection, you know?"

J

Jazzed: *adj.* in an extremely positive frame of mind, psyched up, ready to crank. "I'm like so *jazzed*, OK, these dudes bring three keggers, right, and we like take over the garage, and like it's totally cool cuz my mom and dad are at the spa for the weekend."

Jel: *adj. n.* derogatory term used to describe person with minimal intelligence; short for Jell-O brain; imbecile. "Like Tami fixes me up with this total *jel* from Agri Tech, and all he can talk about is like the future of dairy farming, I'm shurr I care!"

Joanie: *adj.* 1. antiquated, strictly passe, out of date, paleolithic. 2. Liberace. "So I see this total hippie, I mean tie-dye bell-bottoms, a leather vest with nothing on under it, and he's going on about how like the Galleria is sooo psychedelic—talk about *Joanie*, I'm shurr."

K

Keggers: *n.* 1. large container of malt alcoholic beverage. 2. that which is necessary for a bitchen time; a keg of beer. "And like I could die, OK, the garage door opens, and like there's my mom and dad in the Mercedes, and like I'm there with all these dudes and empty *keggers*, and I am so bummed!"

Kill: *adj.* remarkably good, possessing excellence or superior merit; boss. Syn. bitchen, hot, gnarly. "This new store is so hot, like totally rad, like I got these *kill* Guess jeans with a split at the ankle, you know, the kind Courtney has."

L

Lame: *adj.* feeble, flimsy, stupid, dotty. [Not to be confused with physical disability of the same name.] "My algebra teacher is like so *lame* he totally thinks coke is something you drink."

Leather teddy: *n.* 1. intimate garment made famous by Frank Zappa song. 2. a little joke. "I mean it's not like I'm into *leather teddies*—like that's sooo tacky—like I'm totally into my reputation."

Like: *conj.* most commonly used conjunction, often used in place of taking a breath. "I mean like, *like* is like in totally every sentence."

Load: *n.* 1. portion of any illicit substance placed in a bong for the purpose of getting high, esp. bule, ludes, coke. 2. *pl.* people who are loaded, usually found in groups. "Like I totally couldn't believe it, like Todd bonged a *load*, and then like he barfed on Stacey's poodle!"

M

Max, to the: *adj.* greatest, highest, utmost, supreme. "So my dad's getting this hair transplant, and he's like got these scabs and stuff all over his scalp and it's like grody *to the max*."

N

Nerd: *n.* 1. repulsive male person who has attained new heights of offensiveness, distinguished by extreme bad taste. 2. a lousy dresser. Syn. creep, dork, flake, geek, hodad. "I can't believe what a total *nerd* Chrissie's new boyfriend is, his idea of a good time is to sit in front of his home computer and like calculate how many light-years we are from Pluto—the dude is weird, I'm shurr."

O

Ohmigod: *interj.* 1. exclamatory expression that indicates surprise, shock. [Not meant to invoke a Supreme Being.] 2. response to finding a bargain. "*Ohmigod*, the Shoe Showplace is selling metallic flats for like fourteen ninety-nine, fer shurr!"

Orthodontist: *n.* 1. patron saint of Vals. 2. only person whose billing exceeds that of plastic surgeon and dermatologist combined. "I mean, like I'm totally choking on this grody metal thing, and the lame *orthodontist* just smiles, and I go, 'Can I spit or what?' "

P

Pac-Man: *n.* video game involving yellow half-circles, dots, and little blue ghosts accompanied by gobbling noises; fever that strikes people, esp. those under the age of 20; a popular craze often found in video arcades along with Ms. Pac-Man, Centipede, Frogger. "I mean like it was so hairy, like me and Jeff are like totally playing *Pac-Man* for like four hours, right, OK, and like I get this totally grody cramp in my arm."

Party hearty: *interj.* to make merry, frolic, really get down in a group of two or more; used as an imperative only by slimeballs. See *bud, blitzed, buzzed, full-sesh, keggers, load.* "Me and Jeff got way buzzed, right, and like we kinda watched 'Young Doctors in Love' on Betamax, *party hearty!*"

Poindexter: *n.* a brainy geek, a computer nerd, a grind, a bookworm. "Ohmigod, like Hillary's brother is like such a total *Poindexter* he's skipped two grades, I mean like he's in eleventh grade and he doesn't even have hair under his arms!"

Pre-car: *adj.* 1. pertaining to a state prior to the acquisition of a drivers license or a boyfriend with same. 2. that period of early Val adolescence when parents won't let you do anything. 3. virgin. "My mom is like such an airhead, I mean like this bitchen guy calls me and like she tells him I can't go to the Rush concert cuz like I'm *pre-car*."

Q

Quiche: *n.* stupid cheese pie served all too frequently. "Like my mom is having a wine and *quiche* party and like my dad won't eat any cuz he goes, 'It's for bu fus,' and she was way fenced, fer shurr."

R

Rad: *adj.* amazing, wondrous, stunning. [Not pertaining in any way to politics.] "Like Jennifer and I went to this sneak preview, right, and like it's the new Matt Dillon movie, and I mean like Matt is sooo totally *rad*, I could just die!"

Reefdogger: *n.* marijuana cigarette, joint, skinny. "So like I hide these *reefdoggers* in a shoebox, like my mom finds them and she tries to be real cas, right, but then she tells my dad, and like, ohmigod, I'm grounded for a week."

Retard: *n.* any unenlightened person lacking a sense of what is right; ignoramus. Syn. airhead, dork, jel, space cadet. "Like my *retard* little brother borrows my blow drier to like dry his model airplane, right, and so like I can't find it, and I like have to go to school looking like this total zod."

Right: *conj.* used at the end of a sentence, most often as a rhetorical question; requires no answer. "I mean like I'm way edged at that crispo Jeff for like not calling, *right?*"

Rolf: *v.* to vomit, puke, barf, upchuck, toss one's cookies. [Not to be confused with cruel massage-therapy of the same name.] "I mean like I could *rolf*, my mom picks me up at the Galleria, and she's like wearing this skirt and blouse that don't even match, and I was like so embarrassed I could die, I'm shurr."

S

Scarf-out: *v.* to overeat, gorge, guzzle, wolf down, pig out, eat like a horse. "So like I'm on this diet for a week, right, and I lose four pounds, and then I like see Jeff with Kimberly at the beach, and like I'm so totally bummed I *scarf-out*, and like ten Kahlua brownies later I can't even get my jeans zipped!"

Shine: *v.* to completely disregard, overlook, skip. "I dunno, like I totally *shine* algebra class and then I get an A, fer shurr!"

Skanky: *adj.* nauseating, repellent, yukky. Syn. beasty, grody. "I mean like this *skanky* skinhead with black leather and chains and stuff all over goes, 'Wanna see my tattoos?' gag me totally!"

Slimeball: *n.* Aqua Velva geek. Syn. dork, geek, nerd. "Like me and Kimberly go to this bitchen store on Ventura Boulevard, and like the *slimeball* owner is like totally spying on us in the dressing room."

Soc: *n.* from socialite; person who does everything that's socially acceptable to achieve popularity, esp. cheerleaders, class presidents, preppies. "I mean, like every *soc* from Birmingham High was cruising Nathan's deli after the Oingo Boingo concert."

Space cadet: *n.* person who does not have both oars in the water, lacks complete string of lights, is not playing with full deck; a dumb bunny. [Not an astronaut.] "Like we're in Jennifer's new Rabbit convertible, and like she's such a total *space cadet*, we like park at the Galleria, and then she like totally loses the car!"

T

Totally: *adj.* 1. absolutely, quite thoroughly, completely, I mean, like totally. 2. pretty much, sort of, well...maybe a little. 3. word used as filler. "*Totally*, I'm shurr."

Tubular: *adj.* 1. defined by Kimberly D., "That's like really way bitchen, so weird, like totally awesome, you just stamp the ground and go fer it." 2. surfing term for gnarly waves. Syn. awesome, bitchen, rad. "Talk about *tubular*, the Go-Go's are the bitchenest, like they're Vals to the max!"

Tude: *n.* attitude, stance; generally negative. "My English teacher has like this total *tude*, the airhead, he goes like, 'Tiffany, I think you talk funny.' I'm shurr, I'm shurr!"

Twinky: *n.* cute, nubile young person between ages of 13 and 18, usually female; often found in groups. "I mean like this *twinky* must have spent like her total allowance for a month, I mean she buys metallic shoes, metallic belt, metallic headband, I mean like I bet she even chews metallic gum!"

Twitchen: *adj.* complimentary term meaning very good. [Not to be confused with spasmodic jerking.] "I mean like Jeff is wearing this leather jacket with shoulder pads and he looks sooo bitchen *twitchen*, right, like he's out of *GQ* or something."

U

Ugly: *adj.* 1. what Valley girls are not. 2. profoundly unattractive. 3. of a troublesome nature. "Like without my makeup I don't look *ugly* or anything, except for this one zit that is so gross, like I don't want to go out in public or anything."

GOD BLESS OUR MALL

V

Valley: *n.* **1.** orig. a 26 sq. mile geographical area in northern Los Angeles; the San Fernando Valley. **2.** general term used to describe any suburban locale where teenagers congregate to spend billys. **3.** a state of mind. "Like being a *Val* is so tubular, like I go into this record store and this gnarly dude goes, 'Are you a *Val* for real?' and like I just smile cuz like, OK, what could a *Valley* dude want more than a real *Valley* girl?"

W

Way: *adj. adv.* often used in place of totally; extremely, very, really. "I mean we like had this *way* cranking bud sesh and like listened to AC/DC and watched *Mommie Dearest* with the sound off."

X

Xlnt: *adj.* 1. short for excellent, pronounced *zlint*. 2. term used to describe a car you are selling. 3. brand of tamales favored by some Vals. "Like I read this used car ad to my dad, 'Rbt cnvrt, 5 spd, am/fm cass, nu trs, nu brks, lo pymts, *xlnt* cond.' and like I totally beg!"

Y

Yukky: *adj.* that which might cause one to gag with or without a spoon; sickening, icky. "So like I'm getting this pedicure, at the Nail Salon, right, and this crispo manicurist goes, 'Like honey you've got a lot of toe jam,' and, ohmigod, it was sooo *yukky*."

Zappa, Frank and **Moon Unit Zappa:** Frank Zappa, father of The Mothers of Invention, and Moon Unit, daughter of the father of The Mothers of Invention, are members of the bebop elite. They immortalized Vals in the song "Valley Girl."

Zit: *n.* a hideously protuberant excrescence, embarrassing pustule; a pimple. "So like one day before the prom I get this totally grody *zit*, and like I go to Dr. Bubo and like I get this amazing *zit* injection, and then it goes away in three hours, like it's a total miracle, fer shurr!"

Zod: *n.* something really weird or totally monstrous; worse than a nerd, a yuck out. "Like I just got my hair streaked, OK, and like Brian throws me in the pool, and like the chlorine turns my hair like totally green, I mean I look like such a *zod*!"

VAL BODY LANGUAGE

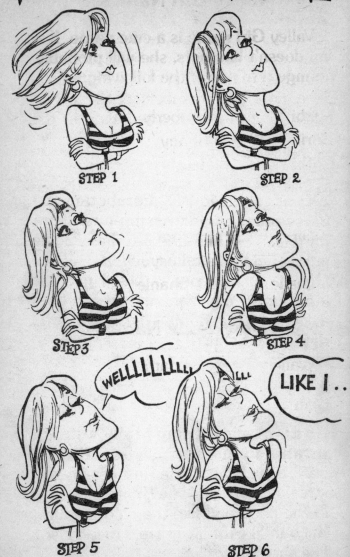

GNARLY VALLEY NAMES

Valley Girl Names

A Valley Girl name is a cute name. If a Val doesn't like hers, she will probably change it to one of the following:

Barbi	Kimberly
Cori	Tiffany
Cathi	Heather
Julie	Stacey
Suzie	Tracey
Tricia	Andrea
Tori	Whitney
Michelle	Stephanie

Valley Dude Names

All Valley dudes are named:

Brian

Jeff

Sean

CLOTHES:
BITCHEN AND JOANIE

A Val wouldn't be caught dead in last year's fashions—or last week's.

Bitchen:	Joanie:
headband	cowboy hat
short shag	long, stringy hair
lots of mascara	false eyelashes
gold chains	too many gold chains
tuxedo blouse	oxford-cloth button down
small leather shoulder-strap bag	oversized fabric pouches
minis	long prairie skirts
opaque panty hose	bare legs
ballet flats	spike heels
one-piece striped maillot swimsuit	string bikini

THE TUBULAR TUBE

Vals love TV. It has helped them through many diets and dudeless Saturday nights. Some of their favorites include:

> *General Hospital*
> *All My Children*
> *The Young and the Restless*
> *Richard Simmons*
> *Fame*
> *Dallas*
> *Dynasty*
> anything on Betamax

Tiffany rates all these malls "bitchen, twitchen."
Did we leave your mall out? If so, fill in the name of your favorite mall.

SOME TOTALLY COOL DUDES

XLNT LISTS

Like everyone else, Valley Girls have their priorities. They like to make lists and cross things off.

Things to do —
1. Make appointment for bikini wax
2. Borrow Heather's copy of G.Q.
3. Find retainer
4. Clean cat box
5. Check out metallic flats on sale at Shoe Connection
6. Start diet
7. Apply for job at Yummy Yogurt.

TUBULAR TIDBITS FROM
Tiffany

What I want for my Sweet Sixteen!
Rabbit convertible
Nose done
Rolex watch
Subscription to G.Q.
Membership in Nautilus
Betamax
Allowance doubled
Totally new wardrobe
A horse!

NO-SWEAT EXERCISE

In general Vals avoid sweating in public.

They will however:

1. ride a bike on a flat surface.
2. take a drive in a Rabbit convertible with the top down for fresh air.
3. buy matching leotard, tights, headband, and leg warmers to make an appearance at a health club.

GO VAL GAL!

VALLEY GIRL
VANITY LICENSE PLATES

ILLINOIS
U RICH 2
LAND OF LINCOLN

OCT 82
4 SHURR
FLORIDA

OCT CALIFORNIA 19 82
U CN B VAL

BIZZEE
NEW YORK OCT 1982

KULDUDE

VALSBMW

VALSPK

2CRANKN

4AVAL

GAGMEE

I8 2MCH

2HOTT4U

QUICHE

VALSKAR

TIFNEE

MERCEDZZ

DADDYZ

WAYRAD

4UHUNY

URSOSLO

BILLEEZ

TAMMEE

L8AGN

2THEMAX

BUFF VALLEY
BUMPER STICKERS

HONK! IF YOU LOVE SHOPPING!

HAVE YOU HUGGED YOUR VAL TODAY?

1 NUCLEAR BOMB CAN BLOW UP THE WHOLE SHOPPING MALL!!

I ♥ BILLYS

CRANKING CAREERS

Someday Daddy will stop paying the bills. Since she needs to earn serious billys, the wise Val considers her career options carefully. They are:

1. Get an MBA.
2. Get a real estate license.
3. Become a model.

THE HAIRY VALLEY-GIRL DIET

For Vals dieting is easy. They do it all the time.

SUNDAY		Calories
Phone fast.	Stay in room, talk on phone.	0

MONDAY		
Breakfast	4 grapes, ½ Diet Pepsi	12
Lunch	½ stick Trident	0
Dinner	1 large lettuce leaf w/lemon juice	2

TUESDAY		
Breakfast	1 Diet Pepsi	1
	1 roll sugarless mints	40

		Calories
Lunch	4 nacho-flavored Dorito chips	30
Dinner	1 can dietetic dumplings	200

WEDNESDAY

Breakfast	2 clove cigarettes, 1 cup black coffee	0
Lunch	1 dill pickle from Kimberly's lunch	86
Dinner	1 whole watermelon	200

THURSDAY

Breakfast	1 cup black coffee, ¼ jelly donut	40
Lunch	1 can lobster paste	100
Dinner	5 portions peach dietetic ice cream	100

FRIDAY		Calories
Breakfast	1 slice cold pizza	200
	1 diet Dr Pepper	0
Lunch	½ cup low-cal cottage cheese	100
	1 Reese's Peanut Butter cup	92
Snack	6 jalapeño jelly beans	72
Dinner	1 8-oz. container piña colada yogurt	210
	1 bag Cheetos	640

SATURDAY

Breakfast	1 head iceberg lettuce	65
Brunch	2 Egg McMuffins	704
Snack	1 lemon-yogurt smoothie	200

		Calories
Lunch	Weight Watchers Cannelloni Florentine	448
Snack	1 pint Häagen-Dazs chocolate-chocolate-chip ice cream w/ 1 oz. low-cal Nutridiet syrup	1005
Dinner	fettucine alfredo	800
	mousse pie (Mom's birthday)	369
Midnight Snack	½ frozen Sara Lee cheese cake	425

SUNDAY

Phone fast.	Stay in room, talk on phone. *Barf me out!!*	0

THE HONORARY VALS

PRINCESS DI

BROOKE   CHERYL   OLIVIA

YOUR PICTURE GOES HERE

GO·GO's

THE ULTIMATE VAL TEST

Does skanky mean something bad or good? Can a cool dude be hot? Take this test, and earn your Val diploma.

Part 1
Reading Comprehension

Mark **T** for True, **F** for False

1. ____ Minis are skanky.
2. ____ Rick Springfield is a box boy at the bonerama.
3. ____ A coaster is a dish or tray placed under glasses to protect the table from moisture.
4. ____ If Tiffany doesn't get a fill, she will look like a gorilla.
5. ____ Encino means "oak" in Spanish.
6. ____ Tiffany's algebra teacher walks with a limp.
7. ____ Sean is a real nice guy.
8. ____ Sheryl's mom is like a total space cadet.
9. ____ Keggers are short pants.
10. ____ Jennifer has a Datsun pickup.

11. _____ Aqua Velva geeks wear really nice boots with zippers.

12. _____ Zits are totally grody.

13. _____ Dr. Bubo is an orthodontist.

14. _____ Tiffany's father really likes quiche.

15. _____ If Tracey gets a zit injection, she will look exactly like Olivia Newton-John.

16. _____ Hodads polish their surfboards with bikini wax.

17. _____ A twinky is a small cream-filled cupcake.

18. _____ Todd barfed on Stacey's poodle.

19. _____ Tiffany's father has scabs on his head.

20. _____ Reefdoggers are a favorite dish at Nathan's deli.

Part 2
Matching

Match the items in the first column with those in the second.

1. geek

2. bong

3. nose job

4. hodad

5. grody to the max

6. ders

7. beige

8. nerd

9. Aqua Velva geek

10. slimeball

11. diet snack

12. ho-ho

13. hot car

14. Joanie

15. tacky

16. shopping

17. twisted headband

a. "surf's up"

b. fat girl

c. any tattoo

d. one who slithers

e. Val hat

f. a way of life

g. sweet sixteen gift

h. Rabbit convertible

i. zits

j. lousy dresser

k. bule

l. a kind of job

m. Liberace

n. discount toupee

o. Häagen-Dazs

p. school

q. wimp

Part 3
Multiple Choice

1. A traditional Valley Girl name is:

    a. Mildred
    b. Ruby
    (c.) Tami
    d. Gertrude
    e. all of the above

2. A traditional Valley Dude name is:

    a. Herman
    b. Boyd
    c. Arnold
    (d.) Sean
    e. all of the above

3. The Valley is:

    a. the shortest distance between two points
    b. a scenic glen populated by well-dressed teens
    c. a state of mind
    d. northern Los Angeles
    (e.) all of the above

4. A favorite Val band is:

a. The Coasters
b. The Snot Puppies
c. Harry Owens and the Royal Hawaiians
d. AC/DC
e. all of the above

5. A Val heartthrob is:

a. Barry Manilow
b. Wayne Newton
c. Erik Estrada
d. Rick Springfield
e. all of the above

6. A Val wouldn't be caught dead in:

a. a girdle
b. speech therapy
c. the arms of a nerd
d. jail
e. all of the above

7. A staple of the Val diet is:

a. bean sprouts
b. carrot sticks
c. sugarless gum
d. broiled fish
e. all of the above

8. For a Val, school is:

   a. a profound challenge
   b. no problem
   c. a deeply gratifying experience
   d. a place to socialize
   e. all of the above

9. For her sweet sixteen a Val wants:

   a. an autographed picture of Ed McMahon
   b. a face lift
   c. stilts
   d. a horse
   e. all of the above

10. Poindexter is a:

   a. brainy geek
   b. Valley hunting dog
   c. new type of diet pill
   d. plate for stupid cheese pie
   e. all of the above

11. A bud sesh implies:

   a. planting tulips
   b. a full day at school
   c. pot party
   d. jam session
   e. all of the above

12. Vals want to grow up to be:

    a. space cadets
    b. theoretical mathematicians
    c. models
    d. orthodontists
    e. all of the above

13. A Val term that is not related to vomiting is:

    a. barf me out
    b. rolf
    c. gag me with a spoon
    d. dermatologist
    e. all of the above

14. A basic element in Val life is:

    a. research grants
    b. head lice
    c. spiritual growth
    d. credit cards
    e. all of the above

Answer Key

Answers to Part 1 Reading Comprehension

1. F, 2. F, 3. F, 4. F, 5. T, 6. F, 7. F, 8. T, 9. F, 10. F, 11. T, 12. T, 13. F, 14. F, 15. F, 16. F, 17. F, 18. T, 19. T, 20. F

Answers to Part 2 Matching

1. q, 2. k, 3. g, 4. a, 5. i, 6. l, 7. p, 8. j, 9. n, 10. d, 11. o, 12. b, 13. h, 14. m, 15. c, 16. f, 17. e

---

Answers to Part 3 Multiple Choice

1. c, 2. d, 3. e, 4. d, 5. d, 6. e, 7. c, 8. b, d, 9. d, 10. a, 11. c, 12. c, 13. d, 14. d

> If you've managed to score at all, our headbands are off to you. Please fill in your name on the way rad Honorary Val Diploma, like OK, right, fer shurr, fer shurr!

SHOPPUS MALLUS ES BONERAMUS

MCMLXXXII

This certifies that

Angelica Hawke
Name of Reader

has completed a course in

VALSPEAK

and is entitled to all the rights, honors, and privileges here and everywhere as an

HONORARY VAL

Instructor: Tiffany

Witness: _____
(must be under 21)

Date of Completion _Nov. 1, 1982_